ATE DUE

Jason Kidd

Additional Titles in the Sports Reports *Series*

Andre Agassi
Star Tennis Player
(0-89490-798-0)

Troy Aikman
Star Quarterback
(0-89490-927-4)

Roberto Alomar
Star Second Baseman
(0-7660-1079-1)

Charles Barkley
Star Forward
(0-89490-655-0)

Terrell Davis
Star Running Back
(07660-1331-6)

Tim Duncan
Star Forward
(0-7660-1334-0)

Dale Earnhardt
Star Race Car Driver
(0-7660-1335-9)

Brett Favre
Star Quarter Back
(0-7660-1332-4)

Jeff Gordon
Star Race Car Driver
(0-7660-1083-X)

Wayne Gretzky
Star Center
(0-89490-930-4)

Ken Griffey, Jr.
Star Outfielder
(0-89490-802-2)

Scott Hamilton
Star Figure Skater
(0-7660-1236-0)

Anfernee Hardaway
Star Guard
(0-7660-1234-4)

Grant Hill
Star Forward
(0-7660-1078-3)

Michael Jordan
Star Guard
(0-89490-482-5)

Shawn Kemp
Star Forward
(0-89490-929-0)

Mario Lemieux
Star Center
(0-89490-932-0)

Karl Malone
Star Forward
(0-89490-931-2)

Dan Marino
Star Quarterback
(0-89490-933-9)

Mark McGwire
Star Home Run Hitter
(0-7660-1329-4)

Mark Messier
Star Center
(0-89490-801-4)

Reggie Miller
Star Guard
(0-7660-1082-1)

Chris Mullin
Star Forward
(0-89490-486-8)

Hakeem Olajuwon
Star Center
(0-89490-803-0)

Shaquille O'Neal
Star Center
(0-89490-656-9)

Gary Payton
Star Guard
(0-7660-1330-8)

Scottie Pippen
Star Forward
(0-7660-1080-5)

Jerry Rice
Star Wide Receiver
(0-89490-928-2)

Cal Ripken, Jr.
Star Shortstop
(0-89490-485-X)

David Robinson
Star Center
(0-89490-483-3)

Barry Sanders
Star Running Back
(0-89490-484-1)

Deion Sanders
Star Athlete
(0-89490-652-6)

Junior Seau
Star Linebacker
(0-89490-800-6)

Emmitt Smith
Star Running Back
(0-89490-653-4)

Frank Thomas
Star First Baseman
(0-89490-659-3)

Thurman Thomas
Star Running Back
(0-89490-445-0)

Chris Webber
Star Forward
(0-89490-799-9)

Tiger Woods
Star Golfer
(0-7660-1081-3)

Steve Young
Star Quarterback
(0-89490-654-2)

SPORTS REPORTS

Jason Kidd
Star Guard

Valerie A. Gray

Enslow Publishers, Inc.
40 Industrial Road   PO Box 38
Box 398   Aldershot
Berkeley Heights, NJ 07922   Hants GU12 6BP
USA   UK
http://www.enslow.com

*This book is dedicated to everyone
who made this dream come true.*

Copyright © 2000 by Valerie A. Gray

All rights reserved.

No part of this book may be reproduced by any means without the written permission of the publisher.

Library of Congress Cataloging-in-Publication Data

Gray, Valerie A.
    Jason Kidd: star guard / Valerie A. Gray.
       p. cm. — (Sports reports)
    Includes bibliographical references and index.
    Summary: Profiles the personal life and basketball career of Jason Kidd, the star point guard, from his college days in California to his professional career with the Dallas Mavericks and Phoenix Suns.
    ISBN 0-7660-1333-2
    1. Kidd, Jason—Juvenile literature. 2. Basketball players—United States—Biography. [1. Kidd, Jason. 2. Basketball players.] I. Title. II. Series.
GV884.K53 G72 2000
796.323'092—dc21
[B]
                                                              99-054581

Printed in the United States of America

10 9 8 7 6 5 4 3 2 1

To Our Readers:
All Internet addresses in this book were active and appropriate when we went to press. Any comments or suggestions can be sent by e-mail to Comments@enslow.com or to the address on the back cover.

Photo Credits: Andrew D. Bernstein/NBA Photos, pp. 54, 64; Barry Gossage/NBA Photos, pp. 10, 18, 24, 29, 42, 72, 78; Juan O'Campo/NBA Photos, p. 47; Noren Trotman/NBA Photos, p. 37; Rocky Widner/NBA Photos, p. 81; Sam Forencich/NBA Photos, pp. 68, 87, 90; Sandy Tenuto/NBA Photos, p. 57.

Cover Photo: Sam Forencich/NBA Photos

Contents

1. Giving 100 Percent 7
2. Evolution of a Point Guard 13
3. College Hoops 21
4. Drafted by the Mavericks 33
5. The Impact Player 51
6. A Classic Point Guard 61
7. Another Playoff Run 75
8. The Kidd's Bright Future 83

Chapter Notes 93

Career Statistics 101

Where to Write 102

Index 103

Chapter 1
Giving 100 Percent

When Jason Kidd plays basketball, he sacrifices his body to hunt down loose balls, steals, and rebounds. He drives down the lane without fear. It is not too surprising, then, that he played even when he had the flu. On April 24, 1999, when the Phoenix Suns played the Houston Rockets, Kidd was not sure he was up to playing that day. He did not have the opportunity to warm up before the game, but he did not want to be an observer. So he decided to give playing a try. The game was important to the Suns.

Playing with the flu was not the only obstacle that Kidd had to overcome. As the game progressed, Kidd's pain and injuries increased. In the first quarter, Scottie Pippen poked him in the eye. Kidd also twisted his ankle in the first quarter. Although Kidd was sick, he still had his wits. In one play in the first half, forward Danny Manning of the Suns was double-teamed by Charles Barkley and guard Cuttino Mobley of the Rockets. To escape the defense of the Rockets, Manning tossed a bounce pass to Kidd. Mobley raced over to defend Kidd. Kidd set himself to put up the shot beyond the foul line, in three-point range. But instead of putting up the shot, Kidd pump faked Mobley, drove to the basket, and put in a fadeaway jump shot that hit the rim once and swooshed in. At the half, the Suns were up 53–36. Jason Kidd had 17 points and 10 assists. This was the first game of the season in which the Suns had such a huge lead over an opponent at the half. But the Rockets were not going to give up easily. Little by little, the Rockets staged a comeback, led by Scottie Pippen. A three-pointer by Pippen made the score 62–50 with more than six minutes to go in the third quarter.

Later in the quarter, Kidd showed no signs of feeling ill when he flew into a table, going after a loose ball. His arm smashed against a television monitor that was on the table, leaving him with a bruised left elbow. He left the game with 1:30 left in the third quarter to get X rays of his elbow.

Kidd was down but not out. With 9:19 remaining

FACT

Jason Kidd plays such an aggressive and fast-paced game that he sometimes has to sit on a stool when he showers after the game because he is too tired to stand.

in the game, Kidd returned. The X rays on his elbow did not show any serious damage. Even with his injuries and illness, Kidd was still able to put up impressive numbers with 22 points, 14 assists, and 10 rebounds, leading the Suns to a 95–71 victory. The Rockets' 71 points were the third-lowest point total allowed by the Suns in franchise history.

The win was the sixth win in a row at home for the Phoenix Suns. Kidd said of the win, "It was a big game for us, and the team played extremely well. Rex [Chapman] and everybody [were] knocking down shots, so that made it a lot easier on me."[1]

Kidd's dedication and superior play led to his being named the NBA Player of the Month for April 1999. His record numbers, such as 7 triple doubles in the season, and many contributions to the Suns, were instrumental in his being selected as a member of the 1999 USA Basketball Men's Senior National Team. Kidd's teammates included Vin Baker of the Seattle SuperSonics; Tim Duncan of the San Antonio Spurs; Kevin Garnett of the Minnesota Timberwolves; a fellow Sun, Tom Gugliotta; Tim Hardaway of the Miami Heat; Allan Houston of the New York Knicks; Gary Payton of the Seattle SuperSonics; and Steve Smith of the Atlanta Hawks. The National Team participated in the 1999 Americas Olympic Qualifying Tournament held in

Despite suffering from the flu and a bruised elbow, Jason Kidd proved he had a lot of heart when he posted 22 points, 14 assists, and 10 rebounds in a defeat of the Rockets in 1999.

San Juan, Puerto Rico, from July 14 to 25. Being chosen for the National Team was an honor for Kidd. "I am flattered more than anything to be selected for the qualifying Olympic team. It is an exciting event and I look forward to help represent the U.S."[2]

Jason Kidd knows no other way to play than to give 100 percent of himself all the time.

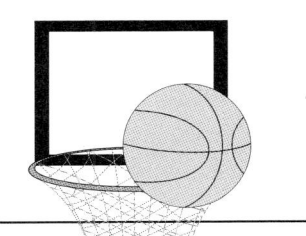

Chapter 2
Evolution of a Point Guard

Jason Frederick Kidd was born in San Francisco, California, on March 23, 1973, to Steve and Anne Kidd. Jason is the oldest of three children. His father was a retired supervisor for Trans World Airlines (TWA), and his mother an assistant programmer for Bank of America. Jason's parents raised their family in a middle-class neighborhood overlooking the scenic hills of San Francisco.

At a very young age, Jason enjoyed the fastbreak—not only on the basketball court but also in other athletic activities. One day, Jason's father took him for a ride on a horse. Instead of riding at a slow trot, Jason wanted to ride at a full gallop. But his father told him that he had to take it slow. "I figured, if you can't go fast, what's the point?" said Jason. "I was never too interested in riding after that."[1]

Jason found out that horseback riding was not for him. He needed to find another sport that did not have speed restrictions. When he was nine years old, he played soccer for his elementary school, St. Paschal's Parochial School. During this time, teachers and coaches were looking for third graders for the basketball team because there were not enough fourth graders interested in playing. Jason decided to give basketball a try. At that point, Jason left the soccer field for the basketball court. This is the time in which Jason sharpened his skills as a guard. In order to fit in and play with the older players, Jason learned to pass. The older kids knew that if they chose Jason, he would pass the ball instead of putting up a shot. Jason was aware at a young age that being an unselfish player was being a team player. "I was always one of the young ones, and for a long time I would be one of the last ones chosen," Jason remembered. "So I learned how to pass."[2]

Jason's skills continued to grow. He developed his basketball skills at the "dunk courts" after school and on the weekends. Children from his neighborhood met there for pickup games. The dunk courts were located at Grass Valley Elementary School. The school was about a quarter of a mile from St. Paschal's. The courts were a popular attraction for children in the area because the rims were around a foot lower than regulation. The baskets were perfect because they enabled the children to get the full effect of the game and give them confidence in developing shots.

In junior high school Jason and his friends would move from various school courts to various parks to practice their games. They wanted to play the best players. Jason spent many hours on the court. "We'd be out there until it was dark and we couldn't see the basket anymore," said Jason. "There was a lot of competition . . . and it was a lot of fun."[3]

During this time, Jason experimented with different ways to deliver the ball. His game advanced so rapidly that when he was fourteen years old, he began receiving recruitment letters from various colleges. His first recruitment letters were from the University of Pittsburgh and the University of Iowa. Jason said, "I hadn't even taken my first high school class yet. I was flattered, but I was thinking, already?"[4] This was just a taste of what Jason could expect. At one point, the recruitment frenzy was so crazy that Jason's parents restricted speaking with recruiters to the last Sunday in each month.

FACT

Jason Kidd set his first record when he scored 21 of 30 points during a fourth-grade Catholic League game.

Jason attended St. Joseph of Notre Dame High School in Alameda, California. The name of his high school team was the Pilots. He wore number 32, the number of his basketball idol, Earvin "Magic" Johnson. From the beginning, he was the star of the team.

It was as a member of this team that Jason's popularity began to grow. "Little kids mobbed Jason for autographs before and after games," said his high school coach and history teacher, Frank LaPorte. "And he got letters from people of all ages all over the country."[5]

But with celebrity comes responsibility. When Jason was fifteen years old, one day his parents gave him the responsibility of baby-sitting for his youngest sister, Kim, who was four years old. But Jason wanted to ride his new moped, so he decided to delegate his baby-sitting responsibilities to his sister Denise, who was thirteen years old. While Jason was out enjoying his ride, his parents were at home waiting for his return. "I said good-bye to that moped. And I didn't go out for a long time after that."[6]

Jason and Coach LaPorte had a close relationship. One day, Coach LaPorte mentioned to Jason that he would like to own a Cadillac. Jason had dreamt of making it to the National Basketball

Association (NBA). When Jason was fifteen, he told his coach that if he made it to the NBA, he would buy him a new Cadillac. LaPorte laughed, and Jason filed the promise in his memory.

Jason's junior and senior years were a one-man highlight reel. Said Coach LaPorte, "Whenever you needed a go-to guy, he'd just hit it. I recall one game he scored 20 out of 22 points in the last quarter to win the game for us."[7] Coach LaPorte gave Jason the freedom to do many things on the court. He went after steals and blocks, and he would create passes that would stump the defense.

Jason's high school play for the Pilots was exciting and sparked the interest of basketball fans in the Bay Area. During his senior year at St. Josephs, five of the team games were moved from the gymnasium at St. Joseph to Oakland Coliseum Arena to have more room for the large crowd.

FACT

Jason Kidd helped the Pilots win 122 of 136 games. Several times, he was chosen as America's High School Player.

Jason helped his teammates by giving them on-the-target passes. And he did not get upset each time a teammate missed a shot. Said former Pilots teammate Kim Stone, "He'd put it right there for you, but some of the guys in high school would blow the lay-ups and he was just real patient with everybody."[8]

With unselfish and electrifying plays, Jason led the Pilots to two Division I state championships

When he was in high school, Jason Kidd dreamed of someday playing in the NBA. He even told his coach he would buy him a Cadillac if he ever reached the pros.

during his junior and senior years and was named California's Player of the Year in 1989 and 1990. Jason was the type of player who felt that it was better to give than to receive. Despite this, he finished his high school career with the Pilots with 2,661 points, which in 1991 ranked him the number-six high school boy scorer in California history.

During a game in the 1991 California tournament with less than a minute to play, Jason rebounded the ball, took it up for a lay-up, to put the Pilots in the lead, and then stole the inbound pass, giving the Pilots the victory.

Some coaches and scouts believed that Jason was ready to move to the NBA after high school, but Jason wanted to go to college. In his senior year he narrowed his choices to two: the University of Kansas and the University of California at Berkeley. Both choices had an underlying element—family. Jason's father was born in Plattsburg, Missouri, a small town north of Kansas City. Jason had relatives who still lived in the area. Said Jason of his memories of Plattsburg, "You don't do too much but relax. I just hang out with my cousin. The town is not so big."[9] But Jason decided to attend the University of California at Berkeley. Said Jason of his decision, "It was a life decision. It came down to staying home and letting my parents see me play like they did in high school."[10] California coach Lou Campanelli was glad to have Jason in his lineup.

But before Jason could think about moving on to college and playing for the University of California, he first had to pass the Scholastic Aptitude Test (SAT). His difficulty passing the test was reported in local papers. This was when Jason found out that not only would the public know about his achievements on the court, the public would also know about his failures off the court. After two attempts, he passed the SAT and was bound for the University of California.

Considered by many to be the best high school player ever to have come out of the Bay Area, Jason was ready to take his game to a higher level. The University of California campus was close to home, but Kidd lived in an off-campus apartment that he shared with childhood friend Andre Cornwell. Kidd was a California Bear. He would be the starting point guard for the team.

Chapter 3
College Hoops

The Bay Area of San Francisco, California, includes Oakland, San Francisco, and San Jose. It has a population of approximately 6.8 million and is a professional sports mecca with such teams as the San Francisco 49ers, the Oakland A's, the Golden State Warriors, and the San Francisco Giants. College basketball had never been a huge draw in the Bay Area. That is, not until Jason Kidd came along.

Kidd accumulated a following in the Bay Area because of his rousing style of play in high school. He brought the excitement of college basketball to the area. The attention that Kidd received throughout his school career had always been overwhelming. But when he played as a California

Bear, it reached at an all-time high. Before his college career began, Kidd's parents requested that his access to reporters be limited to postgame interviews so that he could concentrate on his studies and his game.

On December 1, 1992, Kidd made his debut as a California Bear. The Bears played Sacramento State. Because of his fan appeal, the game was moved to the Oakland Coliseum Arena. Kidd did not disappoint the 12,700 fans who gathered there.

Coach Lou Campanelli gave Kidd limited exposure. (He played for just 28 minutes.) But his presence was felt. Cal forward Brian Hendrick said that just having Kidd on the court makes "the whole team a lot better."[1]

At halftime the Bears led, 48–26. Also at the half, Kidd had 8 assists. Everyone could tell Kidd had made the transition from high school hoops to college hoops with ease. On that night, Kidd tied the California record for steals with 6, and had 10 assists and 11 points. His play contributed to the win over Sacramento State, 89–65.

With Kidd leading the team, the Bears were able to achieve various milestones. On December 22, 1992, the undefeated Bears met the undefeated Demon Deacons of Wake Forest. The game was played in front of an overflowing crowd of 15,039 fans at the Oakland Coliseum Arena. With the game tied at 30–30 with 3.4 seconds left in the first half, Kidd wanted to pass the ball to Lamond Murray but decided that he did not have enough time. So beyond the half-court line, Kidd targeted the basket and bull's-eyed the shot, putting Cal up by 3 points. In the third quarter, the Bears continued their showtime play. Cal freshman guard Jerod Haase stole a pass and threw the ball to Kidd crosscourt. Kidd did not have complete possession, but he was able to somehow slap the ball to Murray, who finished the play with a powerful dunk. The crowd jumped out of their seats in disbelief. The score was 43–39. Even when Kidd showed hustle by trying to get a loose ball, the fans gave him a standing ovation. In another play, Kidd lobbed a twenty-foot touch pass to Lamond Murray that fueled a 17-point Bear run.

Although the fans thought Kidd was Superman, he missed 6 of 10 from the field and 4 of 9 from the line. But with Kidd leading the team, the Bears won the game, 81–65. The Bears were undefeated in their first five games; the best Bear start in fifteen years.

The hype and excitement was intense. Cal played in various arenas in the Bay Area to accommodate the crowds. The Bears even played in the Cow Palace in San Francisco. The Cow Palace can

FACT

In 1993, Jason Kidd set the NCAA freshman record for steals with 3.8 per game. In 1994, he led the nation with 9.1 assists per game in his sophomore year. He also became the first Cal player since Russ Critchfield in 1968, to earn First-Team All-American honors.

When he was at the University of California, Kidd's jump shot was inconsistent. Since reaching the NBA, he has worked to improve it.

seat 12,878 basketball fans; however, in recent years, it has held large crowds for concerts, conventions, and shows. So many fans wanted to see Kidd that his game at the Cow Palace was the first college game to be played there in sixteen years. Kidd's subtle but spectacular plays are the ones that can change the outcome of a game. In this short beginning, basketball experts were comparing him to Magic Johnson.

Here is a breakdown of some of Kidd's and Johnson's stats in their first three college games:

Player	Minutes	Field Goals	Points	Rebounds	Assists
Kidd	93	15 of 26	42	14	22
Johnson	106	14 of 30	38	16	36

Kidd suffered his first college injury during his first road trip, on December 29, 1992. He injured his back and a rib when he fell, in a 90–75 loss against James Madison University. On December 30, he had to sit out the game against Cornell, and the Bears felt his absence. The Bears committed 19 turnovers and shot only 36.4 percent. The Bears' style of play changed because Kidd was not in the lineup, and the other players on the team could not adjust. Coach Campanelli was so upset by the loss that he did not conduct a postgame news conference.

Some felt the Bears needed a new perspective; other thought that Campanelli's verbal skills were not helping to develop the players' basketball skills. In any event, Bears coach Lou Campanelli was let go on February 8, 1993. At the time, the Bears had a 10–7 record. Assistant coach Todd Bozeman took over. The Bears found a spark. Under Bozeman, the Bears went 21–9.

In Kidd's first year as a Golden Bear, he led the team to the Sweet 16 of the National Collegiate Athletic Association (NCAA) championships. "Sweet 16" refers to the top sixteen teams to survive the NCAA tournament. Reaching the Sweet 16 means that a team has reached the last eight games of the tournament. To become a part of the Sweet 16, Cal beat the defending NCAA champs, the Duke Blue Devils. For the first scoring play of that game, Kidd set the stage for what was to come. He found Lamond Murray and pitched the ball to him. Murray dunked it for 2 points. But the Devils were not going to lose a chance to defend their title.

With 2:21 remaining in the game, Duke led, 77–76. But another unbelievable play by Kidd gave the Bears the lead and ultimately, the win. Once again, Kidd's target was Murray. Duke's Billy Hurley blocked the pass. Kidd recovered the loose ball, threw the ball up, and scored. Explaining how he recovered the ball, Kidd said, "I just followed my pass."[2] The Bears were on their way to the Sweet 16.

On March 25, 1993, Cal played the Kansas Jayhawks in the NCAA tournament's Midwest Regional Semifinal. The Bears came to win and expected to win. So did the Jayhawks. The Jayhawks were able to adjust and defend the Bears man-to-man. The Jayhawks had inside knowledge of the Bears' playing style. Jayhawks senior guard Rex Walters had played pickup games with Kidd in high school. He, too, was from the Bay area. Walters had also played with several Bears during the summer. The key to the Jayhawks' success would be to keep the ball away from Kidd.

The Bears led, 52–48, early in the second half. But the lead did not bother the Jayhawks. They became more intense. The Bears were confined in their style of play. They got in foul trouble. Kidd fouled out for the first time in the season. The Jayhawks went on an 11-point run that eliminated the hopes of the Bears. The ability to penetrate the offense gave the Jayhawks the win, 82–69.

Kidd finished his last game of the season with 13 points and 10 assists. He hoped for a better year in his sophomore season. "We're young, and we'll be back next season with big smiles on our faces."[3]

Jason Kidd wanted to cap his sophomore year at Cal with an NCAA championship. Along the way the Bears upset teams that were ranked in the top five. On January 30, 1994, the Bears played the number-one-ranked UCLA Bruins. Kidd took control during the fourth period. As well as feeding the ball to his teammates, he scored 9 of the last 11 points for the Bears. Kidd went with the tempo of the game by adjusting to the flow of the game. "I just let the game come to me," said Kidd. "I don't tell myself to take over the game. I go how the pace is going."[4] Kidd's play helped the Bears to a 85–70 victory.

Going into the tournament, Cal was the fifth-seed team, which means that it was regarded as the fifth-best team, among all of the NCAA teams. The Bears played twelfth-seed Wisconsin-Green Bay at Phoenix. Because of their ranking and performance going into the tournament, the Bears were expected to win. The first half of Cal's first-round tournament game did not go as expected. For the first five minutes of the game, the Bears did not score. A Cal run late in the first half had the Bears behind, 32–23.

Wisconsin-Green Bay started the second half with intensity. Realizing that they had to forge an attempt, the Bears made a 22–3 run and barely led Green Bay, 51–50, with 6:42 remaining in the game.

Jason Kidd's experiences as a member of the basketball team for the University of California helped prepare him for the NBA.

But the Bears could not keep the run going. Kidd finished what would be his last college game with 11 rebounds, 7 assists, and 3 steals. Unfortunately, he also had 6 turnovers. Kidd took the loss very personally and blamed himself. "It wasn't dropping for me tonight," Kidd said. "I'm taking the blame for this because it's really my fault."[5]

During his last season at Cal, Kidd discussed with his parents and Bozeman the possibility of turning pro. The Wisconsin-Green Bay upset helped seal his decision. Kidd had mixed emotions about his choice. "I really did not want my college career to end on that note. I'd promised my teammates we'd go to the Final Four. I felt I let us down, and that came into play."[6]

So on Kidd's twenty-first birthday, at a news conference with approximately one hundred reporters present and supported by family and friends, he announced he was no longer a California Golden Bear. Said Coach Bozeman of Kidd's decision, "I think he's ready to accept the challenge of everything that's out there for him."[7]

When asked why he decided to go pro instead of staying at Cal, Kidd replied, "I felt my job here at Cal was finished. I've done everything I can, poured my heart and soul into every game. I thought it was time to try something new and experience a whole new game of basketball, with the best players in the world."[8] For the moment, Kidd gave up graduating from college to become an NBA player.

The months following Kidd's announcement would be personally nerve-racking for him. In a string of mishaps, the spotlight was not on his basketball skills but his off-court actions. In one incident, Kidd was accused of driving over the speed limit when he lost control and crashed his father's new 1994 Toyota Landcruiser into a wall. He was driving two acquaintances home when the accident occurred. After the accident, Kidd left the scene. He was charged with speeding and a hit-and-run accident. He pleaded no contest, was convicted, and was sentenced to two years' probation and one hundred hours of community service, and was fined one thousand dollars. One of Kidd's passengers was charged with suspicion of vandalism, resisting arrest, and public drunkenness.

Jason Kidd's parent's hoped this had been a momentary lapse in judgment. Said his father, Steve, "Jason got into the fast lane with the wrong people. We just hope and pray he's back down to earth."[9]

Kidd hoped that his off-the-court activity would not jeopardize his NBA hopes or give him a bad reputation. Kidd said, "I've got to develop a strategy to deal with this, to protect myself. I've got to find out how to be the real Jason Kidd."[10]

Kidd hoped that moving on from college basketball and becoming a member of an NBA team would help him find his way. Only time would tell how things would work out for Jason Kidd.

Chapter 4
Drafted by the Mavericks

The Cowboys have always been known as the sports team in Dallas, Texas. With numerous Super Bowl wins and players such as Herschel Walker, Emmitt Smith, and Troy Aikman, sports fans there always expected winners from their teams. Others felt that Dallas had enough fans to support not only football but also basketball. In 1980, a franchise agreement was signed that brought basketball to Dallas. Owner Donald Carter paid $12 million for the NBA franchise, and the Mavericks become a member of the NBA's Midwest Division.

As with most new teams, the Mavericks went through an adjustment period. For its first season, the team had 15 wins and 67 losses. During the

1981–1982 season, its second, the team had 28 wins and 54 losses. The team continued to improve and made it to the playoffs for five consecutive seasons. But the 1988–1989 season marked the beginning of a downhill slide. The decline bottomed out during the 1992–1993 season, when the team won only 11 games; the worst record in franchise history. The following season, the team improved its record by only 3 games, winning a total of 14. The Mavericks organization knew that changes needed to be made to energize the offense and bring excitement back to basketball in Dallas.

One positive element of being a losing team is that the odds of receiving a great lottery pick at the NBA draft increase for the following season. Owner Donald Carter and Coach Dick Motta were rebuilding the team and wanted a leader to take the team to the playoffs. They knew that they needed an "impact" player. With the number-two pick in the NBA draft, they had their eyes on Jason Kidd. Kidd attended minicamp with the Mavericks and impressed management. He was also interested in playing for the Mavericks.

NBA scout Don Leventhal's NBA draft report on Kidd included the following:

> Superb play maker. He passes quickly and decisively when he spots the open man. Seems

to have the sixth sense and anticipation that only the truly great players possess. Excellent passer, off the dribble. Runs the fast break extremely well and makes very good decisions.[1]

The 1994 NBA draft was held on June 29 in Market Square Arena in Indianapolis, Indiana. Each year the draft is filled with talented players waiting for their chance at NBA stardom. But the 1994 draft had many big-name players who would later make their mark in the NBA. Players such as Glenn Robinson, Grant Hill, and of course, Jason Kidd were included.

Kidd was the number-two overall draft pick for the Mavericks, behind number-one draft pick Glenn Robinson, picked by the Milwaukee Bucks; and in front of Grant Hill, picked by the Detroit Pistons. Coach Motta's response to picking Kidd included, "When the ball is in his hands, he almost never makes a bad decision."[2]

In a letter sent to Mavericks season-ticket holders, President Norm Sonju wrote, "The thought of Jamal Mashburn, Jim Jackson, and other Maverick players out on the open court with Jason running the fast break is flat-out exciting."[3] The acquisition of Kidd made the Mavericks the second-youngest team in the NBA, second to the Los Angeles Clippers.

FACT

Jason Kidd set a club record for the Mavericks in 1995–1996 with 783 assists and 553 rebounds. He became only the sixth player in NBA history to have more than seven hundred assists and five hundred rebounds in the same season.

Jason Kidd made his NBA debut on November 4, 1994. The Mavericks played the New Jersey Nets in Reunion Arena, the Mavericks' home court. There were a lot of expectations for the Mavericks' number-two draft pick and $54 million rookie. He and his teammates did not disappoint the fans. Kidd had 11 assists, scored 10 points, and nabbed 9 rebounds and 3 steals. The Mavericks won their season opener, 112–103. Kidd's teammates fed off the energy and excitement of a new season. Shooting guard Jim Jackson tied a career-high 37 points. Said Jackson of the experience, "It's great to have somebody on the court who is a true point guard."[4] The opposition was also impressed by Kidd's ability. "Jason has a lot of talent," said New Jersey coach Butch Beard. "He'll be a good one when it's all said and done."[5] Although Kidd's stats were impressive, he expected to accomplish more in his professional career. "This is just the first game in a long career," Kidd said. "To me it was just an average performance."[6]

Kidd accomplished a great deal in his first year. He shined as he played in front of his hometown. On March 13, 1995, the Mavericks played the Golden State Warriors in the Oakland Coliseum Arena; a place that Kidd was very familiar with. Kidd scored a season-high 30 points and recorded 17 assists. The Mavericks won with a final score of

Before he became a Phoenix Sun, Jason Kidd was a member of the Dallas Mavericks. He was selected by the Mavericks with the second pick of the 1994 draft.

130–125. The 130 points were the most the Mavericks scored that season. The victory also ended a four-game losing streak for the Mavericks and was their third victory over the Warriors. Such aggressive play from Kidd led to his being named the NBA Player of the Month for March.

On April 7, 1995, Jason Kidd demonstrated his ability to influence the outcome of a game by making big plays. The Mavericks were up against the Minnesota Timberwolves. The game marked the second consecutive game in which Kidd posted a triple double. A triple double occurs when a player scores in double figures in the categories of points, rebounds, and assists in a game. Kidd's triple double consisted of 11 points, 10 rebounds, and 13 assists. During the first half, Kidd handed 9 assists and grabbed 8 rebounds. Kidd sacrificed points in order to set his teammates up for scoring. The Mavericks won the game, 111–94. Timberwolves assistant coach Mike Schuler attributed the Mavericks' success to Kidd's play. "If they didn't have Jason Kidd, they might not have had that many second shots," said Schuler. [7]

Kidd got his third triple double in a game against the Houston Rockets on April 11, 1995. In this contest the Rockets and the Mavericks battled it out in double overtime. Kidd scored 3 three-pointers in the last 55 seconds of the first overtime that sparked the Mavericks to a victory, 156–147. The game took a lot out of Kidd. "I've never been in a game like this before, and I hope it will be my last," Kidd said. "But it definitely feels good."[8] Kidd finished the game with 11 rebounds and 10 assists. Teammate Jamal Mashburn scored 42 points. Both teams had a total of 28 three-point baskets, which set an NBA record.

As the 1995 regular season was ending, talk grew about who would be named the Rookie of the Year. The focus was on three players: Glenn Robinson, Grant Hill, and Jason Kidd. The winner of the award is determined by 105 news media members who cover the NBA. Each member votes for his or her selection. Many members knew the vote would be close because each player brought unique qualities to his game. Glenn Robinson was a big scorer; Grant Hill was a good all-around player; and Jason Kidd was an impact player. Kidd's style of play ignited the Mavericks and was instrumental in helping the team improve its record from the previous season by 23 games. During his rookie year, Kidd was able to create wins for the team with his passing and rebounding abilities. Kidd's first-year play impressed his coach. Said Motta, "He exceeds every expectation I had for him."[9]

Jason Kidd and Grant Hill had been friends since their high school days. In college, a friendly rivalry began between Cal and Duke. So it was only fitting that both players were named to share the Rookie of the Year honors. It was only the second time in NBA history that two players received corookie honors. The first occurred during the 1970–1971 season when the Boston Celtics' Dave Cowens and the Portland Trail Blazers' Geoff Petrie shared the award. Both players received 43 first-place votes. Hill wanted the rivalry to continue. He said, "It would be nice if we could develop a rivalry in the NBA like the one between Magic Johnson and Larry Bird. I'm sure Jason would like that too."[10]

Jason Kidd's passing ability set up Jimmy Jackson and Jamal Mashburn, establishing them as the thirteenth set of teammates in NBA history to average 24 or more points per game while playing in at least fifty games—and the youngest to accomplish the feat. The threesome was referred to as the "Three J's" (Jason, Jamal, and Jimmy).

With Kidd's success came increased popularity. He appeared on talk shows such as *Regis and Kathie Lee*, *The Tonight Show* with Jay Leno, and *Good Morning America*. There was also a commercial for Nike, and a Dallas-area "The Kidd Meal Deal" commercial for McDonalds.

The fans and the Mavericks organization were excited about the improvement of the team. The Mavericks had come close to making a playoff appearance. But for the 1995–1996 season, the team was expected to gain a playoff spot. The first two months of the season would set the tone for what was to come—a season of ups and downs.

In the season opener, the Mavericks played the Spurs in San Antonio. Jason Kidd dominated the offense with 27 points. Then, the Golden State Warriors came to town for the Mavericks' home opener. For this game, Kidd's rebounding and assists helped the Mavericks win. The Mavericks won the next two games—the best-ever start for the Mavs. Kidd's success put him and the Mavericks in the spotlight.

Although Kidd's strongest skill is not shooting, he continuously tried to improve his scoring percentage from the outside. "When Coach Motta wants me to score, I want the ball. But when other people are scoring, I will get them the ball."[11]

With three young superstars and a town full of expectations, the team started to feel the pressure. The Three J's wanted equal ball time and felt that some players were hogging the ball. This conflict led to a downward spiral for the team. By the second week of December, the Mavericks were 1–5 during a

Kidd and the Pistons' Grant Hill shared Rookie of the Year honors in 1995. It was only the second time in NBA history that two players shared the award.

road trip and had lost a total of eleven of twelve games. In addition, when playing in Miami, half the team came down with food poisoning. This made Kidd wonder, "What else can go wrong?"[12] Kidd summed up the problem with the Mavericks by declaring, "We need to get back to the way it was last year when everyone was loose and relaxed. This year everyone's uptight and taking things too seriously."[13]

Kidd continuously improved on his personal best. On January 30, 1996, Kidd played an entire 48-minute game for the first time in his career. He finished the game with 21 points, 16 rebounds, and 16 assists. He also helped the Mavericks beat the Clippers, 105–101.

Once again, Kidd's success led to comparisons to his childhood idol, Magic Johnson. In response to those comparisons, Kidd replied, "I've still got a long way to go."[14]

In the last game before the All-Star break, Kidd played like an all-star. The Mavs–Utah Jazz game was a double-overtime nail-biter. On an incredible play, Kidd, with his back to the basket, caught a pass from George McCloud, and then miraculously found the boards with an over-the-shoulder look. On another play, Kidd raced down the lane. In midair, he switched hands on the ball and went up

FACT

In 1996, Jason Kidd appeared in the television debut of *Sparks*, a sitcom on the UPN network. He played the fiancé of one of the main characters, Wilma, played by Robin Givens.

for a lay-up. In addition, Kidd set up his teammates, including a pick-and-roll for Loren Meyer, and a drive-and-disk to McCloud, who scored 3 points. Kidd ended the night with 20 points, 4 steals, 4 rebounds, and 25 assists, to set an NBA record for the most assists since Kevin Johnson had done it in April 1994; broke Magic's Reunion Arena record of 24 assists; broke his own personal-best record and the Mavs' franchise record of 18; and tied a Maverick record with 13 assists in the first half. Jason Kidd dreamed of playing in the All-Star Game. "I would love to pass to Karl and Sir Charles and Shawn Kemp and Drexler, and Olajuwon," he said. "That's what's so fun about playing this game is that I get to play with the best players in the world."[15]

Kidd's dream of playing in the All-Star Game came true on February 11, 1996. He was the first Maverick to start an All-Star Game, and the youngest player voted to start by the fans. The East and the West All-Stars met in San Antonio's Alamodome. Many of the players were of the opinion that Kidd should not have received the starting job, even though the fans voted for him. They believed that other players, such as Utah's John Stockton and Seattle's Gary Payton, were more deserving. But Kidd's performance put those opinions to rest.

During his All-Star appearance, Kidd taught others and learned a few things himself. Kidd taught Charles Barkley the importance of running with his head up. He did not want to deliver a no-look pass to Barkley and have the ball hit him in the head. Kidd wondered what Barkley's reaction would be, but Barkley just said, "I hear you."[16]

Kidd also learned a trick or two from Michael Jordan. This was the first time since 1993 that Jordan had played in an All-Star Game, and he did not miss a beat. On one play, Jordan faked out Kidd. "He got me on a give and go," said Kidd. "He showed me he's still the man."[17] After the lesson, both men acknowledged each other with big grins.

One of Kidd's big plays was a behind-the-back pass to Seattle's Shawn Kemp, who put it up for an awesome dunk. In another play, Kidd collaborated with Clyde Drexler and Charles Barkley. Kidd passed to Drexler under the basket, and Drexler passed to Barkley, who put up a lay-up. That collaboration continued on the bench. "I got a kick sitting on the bench talking to Barkley and Clyde Drexler."[18]

Jason Kidd delivered a game-high 10 assists, posted 7 points, grabbed 7 rebounds, and lifted 2 steals. Kidd's reaction to his first All-Star Game was "I had a lot of fun and played a pretty good game."[19]

Another dream of Kidd's came true on February 16, 1996, when he had a chance to play against his idol. This was the first season back for Magic Johnson. He had left following the discovery that he was HIV positive. This was not the first encounter between Kidd and Johnson. They had played each other in summer pickup games and in charity games sponsored by Johnson. However, in their first regular-season meeting, Kidd was in awe, and his statistics in the first quarter proved it. In the first quarter, Kidd missed five field goals and committed five turnovers. In the second quarter, Kidd's passing and blocking were instrumental in helping the Mavericks to a 3-point lead, going into the fourth quarter. But the Lakers, led by Magic, were able to defeat the Mavericks, 119–114. Johnson finished the game with a team-high 30 points, his season best, 11 assists, and 8 rebounds in 31 minutes. Even though the Mavs lost, playing against Magic meant a lot to Kidd. "One of the many dreams I've been living has been fulfilled," Kidd said. "To play against my idol."[20]

The fast-break play of the Mavericks continued to set NBA records. On February 28, 1996, the Mavericks hit 18 three-pointers, to break the record

In the type of performance Phoenix fans would soon hope to see, Jason Kidd had 21 points, 16 rebounds, and 16 assists in a game against the Los Angeles Clippers in 1996.

set by Golden State against Minnesota on April 12, 1995. Twelve of the three-pointers came in the first half, which set a record for the most three-pointers in a half. Kidd contributed 26 points, 12 rebounds, and 12 assists in the 137–120 win over the Denver Nuggets.

Despite the record-breaking statistics and Kidd's All-Star style of play, the Mavericks were unable to improve their record from the previous year. They ended the season with 26 wins and 56 defeats.

Jim Cleamons was hired as head coach in May. Cleamons coached a half-court offense, but Kidd liked the fast break. At the beginning of the 1996–1997 season, Kidd's stats on offense declined. The new coaching system and off-the-court differences with his teammates started to take their toll on Kidd. He felt that his teammates did not share his philosophy of ball sharing. Kidd's father saw the effect it was having on his son. "It was eating him up. He'd go to bed, go to sleep and hope it'd all be over when he woke up."[21] Kidd decided that he had to voice his concerns so that he could get back to playing on a high-performance level. Ultimately, Kidd, Coach Cleamons, and the Mavericks organization had varying opinions on which direction the team should go. The Mavericks franchise wanted to make another major change. So on December 26, 1996, Kidd, along with guard Tony Dumas and center-forward Loren Meyer, was traded to the Phoenix Suns for guard Sam Cassell and forwards Michael Finley and A. C. Green.

Jason Kidd reacted to the trade by saying, "I have to welcome it. Phoenix is a great place to play. At the same time, it's sad because I like playing in Dallas."[22]

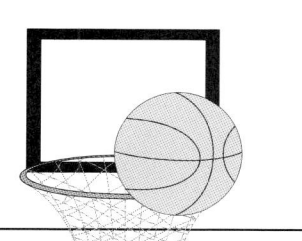

Chapter 5
The Impact Player

The 1996–1997 season was Danny Ainge's rookie coaching season for the Phoenix Suns. His coaching style mirrored Kidd's playing style. Both enjoyed the excitement of the fast break. Ainge looked forward to having Kidd in the lineup and knew the change would only help Kidd's play. "When I first saw Jason play, I never saw anyone more passionate about the game," said Ainge. "This year I didn't see it. We think a change of scenery will rejuvenate him."[1]

The Suns had made a playoff appearance for the past seven seasons. This season the team got off to a dismal 0–13 start. Ainge knew that Kidd would have an impact on the Suns for this season and for years to come. "This is for our future. Jason Kidd is a franchise player. He's a perennial all-star."[2] Kidd made his debut as a Sun on December 28, 1996, in a road trip against the Vancouver Grizzlies. In the first 20 minutes of the game, Kidd made a sudden impact. He racked up 9 assists and 7 rebounds. But the momentum that he built was abruptly stopped. Kidd suffered a hairline fracture of the his right collarbone. The Suns went on to win the game, 103–98. However, Kidd's injury would sideline him for six weeks.

Kidd recovered from this injury and debuted again on February 14, 1997, against the Los Angeles Clippers in the America West Arena. Ainge had to alter his lineup for the addition of Kidd. Kevin Johnson had been the point guard. Johnson was shifted to shooting-guard starter. Some fans worried that Kevin Johnson and Kidd would not be able to connect. There was no need to worry. Johnson played at both the point- and shooting-guard positions and scored 27 points and had 8 assists. Kidd's presence elevated Johnson's play.

The Suns implemented a new rule that indicated only wives, not girlfriends, were allowed to ride the team plane. Coach Ainge joked that was the reason that Kidd decided to get married. On February 21, 1997, in a brief civil ceremony, Kidd married his girlfriend, Joumana Samaha. Suns assistant coach Paul Silas was his best man. Kidd chose Silas to be his best man because "he's been married 30 years. He sets a good example," Kidd said.[3] The couple planned a full ceremony on August 31.

Kidd's first appearance against the Mavericks since the trade occurred on March 2, 1997. Kidd admitted to being emotional about the encounter. This emotion seemed to filter through the whole team. In the third quarter the Suns were trailing by 27 points. Kidd said, "I was trying to force things early on."[4]

But Kidd and the Suns chipped away at the lead. With seconds on the clock, Kidd barreled down the lane, attracting the defense, hurled a pass to Wayman Tisdale, who put in a lay-up that barely beat the buzzer and gave the Suns a 109–108 win. Kidd said of the victory, "Emotionally, this was a good game for me."[5]

In April 1997 Kidd realized that he and the team had a chance to make it to the playoffs. With ten games left in the season, he started to dream of the possibility. "Every time you leave training camp, your goal is to reach the playoffs," Kidd said.[6] After three years in the NBA, Kidd's dream came true.

When Kidd reentered the lineup after his injury, the Suns' record was greatly improved. In their last

FACT

Jason Kidd enjoys listening to rhythm and blues music. His favorite artists include Chante Moore and the Isley Brothers. He also enjoys playing video games.

The Suns began the 1996–97 season by losing their first 13 games. Obviously in need of some help, they traded for Jason Kidd on December 26, 1996.

32 games, the Suns won 23 and finished the season with a 40–42 record.

The concern about Johnson and Kidd was unfounded. Ainge said, "Both of them had to make some adjustments. But they've really been willing to work with each other. They've both made sacrifices."[7] Both were key in the Suns' success. "I know what he needs to do and vice versa. We've been playing off each other very well. I love playing with him," Kidd said of Johnson.[8]

On April 24, 1997, the Suns played the Seattle SuperSonics in the first round of the playoffs. Rex Chapman was in the zone and led the Suns to a 106–101 victory.

In the second game, the Sonics were able to adjust to the Suns' offense. The Sonics got off to an intense start. They were on their home court and took advantage of the supporting fans. The Sonics held a shooting clinic as they hit 14 of 19 shots, including 3 three-pointers. Shawn Kemp, Gary Payton, and Detlef Schremp alone scored 29 of 33 points. At the end of the first quarter, the Sonics led, 33–8. The Suns' starters made only 3 of 21 shots in the first half. Things did not improve for the Suns. Even Coach Ainge was ejected from the game for walking on the court to challenging the referee's calls. The Suns were out of sync and never found a playing groove.

Kidd went zero for seven from the field. His first points came late in the fourth quarter due to free throws. He finished with 8 assists. Johnson finished with 6 points and 2 assists. In the end, the game was a blowout, 122–78. Said Seattle coach George Karl of the win, "You know KJ and Kidd are not going to go 1 for 19 ever again, probably. We were fortunate to catch them on a bad night."[9]

The Suns knew they had to regroup for Game 3. But starting out, the Sonics were just as intense as they had been for Game 2. With less than five minutes remaining in the first quarter, the Sonics had a 31–16 lead. Coach Ainge knew that he had to do something to get the Suns back in the game. So he implemented his "four on the floor" offense, which consists of four guards: Kevin Johnson, Wesley Person, Rex Chapman, and Jason Kidd. This offensive formation came as a surprise to the Sonics, and they could not adjust. Kidd concentrated on the small plays that changed the outcome of the game. He finished with 4 steals, 6 rebounds, 10 assists, and 7 points. The Suns won, 110–103. The Suns led the series, 2–1. The team was looking forward to moving to the second round of the playoffs, where the Houston Rockets were waiting.

But first, the Suns had to win Game 4, and both teams felt the urgency. From the beginning, the

With Jason Kidd's help, the Suns overcame their 0–13 start to make the playoffs. Even though the team lost in the first round to Seattle, it was the first team in league history that lost 13 or more consecutive games and still reached the postseason.

Suns' fans knew they were going to witness a classic game. It was survival of the fittest for both teams. The game came down to the last 4.3 seconds in the fourth quarter. The Sonics led, 106–104. Kidd lobbed an on-target pass to Chapman, who put up a miracle running shot that tied the score at 106–106 and revived the hopes of the Suns. But the Suns could not keep the momentum going. The Sonics retained their groove in overtime and did not let go. The final score was 122–115. Said Ainge of the thriller," Oh wow, that was an awesome game, but the wrong guys won. Let's go play Game 5. Bring 'em on. We feel confident."[10] The series was coming down to a fifth and deciding game.

Game 5 was held in Key Arena in Seattle. In the opening quarter, the Suns trailed by 22 points. In the end, the deficit was too much to overcome. The Sonics were able to control Kidd, Chapman, and the rest of the Suns. The final score was 116–92, Sonics.

Although the Suns did not get beyond the first round of the playoffs, they became the first team in NBA history to have lost thirteen or more straight games during the regular season and still make the playoffs. Yet another testament to Jason Kidd's impact and ability to turn a team around was evident.

After the Suns' playoff run, Kidd went to California to fulfill the promise he had made to his coach when he was fifteen years old. Kidd presented his high school coach, Frank LaPorte, with a new aqua-green Cadillac. Said LaPorte, "When a 15-year-old kid makes a promise, you don't really expect him to keep it, but he did."[11]

On August 30, 1997, Kidd and his wife, Joumana, renewed their vows in a formal ceremony. The ceremony took place at St. Mary's Cathedral in San Francisco. Approximately five hundred fifty guests helped the couple celebrate. The couple spent their honeymoon in Paris, France.

The Suns had big expectations for the upcoming season. Of course, the team wanted to make the playoffs, but this time, it wanted to go beyond the first round. Another expectation was the development of Jason Kidd and Antonio McDyess as a twosome to be reckoned with. The hope was for the two to be as powerful as Karl Malone and John Stockton. The skills of each player complemented the other's. Also, the Suns signed George McCloud to a one-year contract. The Suns believed that this was a good acquisition, not only because of his level of play, but also because Kidd and McCloud had developed a friendship when they were both with the Mavericks that would be displayed on the court. The Suns were ready for the 1997–1998 season.

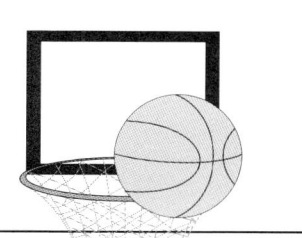

Chapter 6
A Classic Point Guard

Jason Kidd brings many dimensions to his role as a point guard. He can fake out the opposing player with his no-look passing. He can conduct his teammates by setting up the offense. Kidd's ability to deflect passes and run down more loose balls than any other player in the NBA contribute to the success of the Suns.

One of the things that makes Kidd a superior passer is his excellent vision on the court. He sees the action on the entire court and accurately passes the ball to his teammates from all areas of the court. He enjoys having control of the ball and making the decision to pass. "I'm not a shoot-first-and-ask-questions-later guard. I like to pass."[1] Kidd's first full season as a Sun proved he was, indeed, a classic point guard.

The Suns broke the curse of the previous season's 0–13 start by winning their 1997–1998 season opener against the Los Angeles Clippers. Kidd covered the Clippers' Darrick Martin like a shadow for most of the game, preventing Martin from scoring on any of his nine attempts. Kidd's final tally was 16 assists, 14 rebounds, 6 steals, and 6 points. The Suns used Kidd, Johnson, and Steve Nash in the three-point-guard lineup that kept the Clippers off balance. The Suns were able to score 22 points on 19 Clippers' turnovers, to post a 110–100 victory.

Jason Kidd was the first to admit that his scoring percentage needed improvement. He worked regularly with assistant coach Frank Johnson. For added help, Kidd's wife, Joumana, kept files on Kidd's progress. Her files included charts, comparisons between Kidd and players such as Penny Hardaway, Grant Hill, and Gary Payton. Kidd was teased by his teammates. But the teasing was easier than Joumana's comments. Said Kidd, "She's my toughest critic of all. It's tough to ride home after games some nights. She doesn't hold back on me. But I'll listen to her more than [to] a lot of people."[2] Joumana's assistance seemed to pay off.

In the first nine games of the season, Kidd's field-goal, three-point, and free-throw percentages were all above his career highs. Said Coach Johnson, "She makes sure he puts in his work. If I want Jason to work on something, I go to her."[3]

It had been a year since the trade between the Mavericks and the Suns, and the impact on both teams was evident. Since the trade, the Mavericks had 20 wins and 63 defeats. Since the Suns had acquired Kidd, the team had 47 wins and 31 defeats. On January 1, 1998, Kidd entered the Reunion Arena in Dallas for the third time since the trade. The experience still felt strange to him. "I think it's always going to be weird to come here. I thought I was always going to be a Maverick, but things aren't always set in stone."[4] The Mavericks led, 63–54, in the third quarter, but the Suns replied with a 16–3 run to end the quarter. With less than two minutes remaining and the Suns up, 85–84, Nash hit a two-point basket. Kidd sealed the win by hitting 4 free throws in the final seventeen seconds, to make the score 91–85. The Suns were able to contain the Mavericks in the final 9 seconds of the game. Jason Kidd finished the game with his second triple double of the season for 20 points, 12 rebounds, and 14 assists. Kidd reflected on his experience in Dallas and the Three J's by saying they were "three young

Jason Kidd is known as a classic point guard because he is an excellent passer. He would rather pass the ball to a teammate than shoot it.

guys who all wanted to win and would have done anything to win. But at the same time we just didn't know how to do it and we all got frustrated."[5]

For motivation and to reinforce his idea of what a team player should be, Kidd watched the championship tapes of Danny Ainge, Larry Bird, and the other Celtics players, and he talked to Ainge about being on a championship team.

Kidd appreciated his multitalented teammates because they offered a lot of diversity in plays. "It's like point guard heaven," Kidd said. "My job is to get the ball to the right person at the right time."[6] Kidd believed he was on target for this season to be his best. He was consistent in all areas of his play. He was the go-to guy for the Suns. Said Ainge, "Jason finds ways to win."[7]

Jason Kidd has tried different techniques to give his game an edge. He is right-handed, but throughout the years, he practiced lay-ups leading with his left hand. Doing so gives him the ability to lead off with either leg, an ability that enables Kidd's diversity of movement.

Coach Ainge always looks for an edge in winning. One edge that he found was in studying the personality of his players. He contacted Jonathan Niednagel who has established various personality types: E—extroversion; I—introversion; S—sensing;

FACT

Jason Kidd enjoys collecting vintage cars. His collection includes four Mercedes, a Lambretta, and an Impala that he restored.

N—intuition; T—thinking; F—feeling; J—judging; P—Perceiving. Ainge categorized Kidd, Larry Bird, Michael Jordan, and John Stockton as having the same personality types—ISTP. The common denominator for these players is that they are all competitive. Although Coach Ainge does not rely 100 percent on the personality analysis, he believes the tool is valuable because "it makes me more understanding of the strengths and weaknesses of players."[8]

Kidd's talents and consistent style of play were noticed by the NBA's Western Conference coaches. They picked Kidd to represent the West in the All-Star Game. Said Kidd of the selection, "This is a great, great honor."[9] The game was held on February 8, 1998. Jason Kidd was the only Sun named to the All-Star team, but he said that his selection was also a reflection of his teammates. Kidd represented his teammates well. He played 19 minutes and had 9 assists. For one of his assists, Kidd brought oohs and aahs from the fans at Madison Square Garden with a one-handed scoop pass to Los Angeles Laker Eddie Jones, who put it in with a stylish dunk. Kidd also briefly guarded Michael Jordan during the game. The East won the game, 135–114, but it was a great experience for Jason Kidd.

Jason Kidd went on to show that his wife's help in increasing his shooting percentage had paid off. On February 14, 1998, he matched his season high with 29 points against the San Antonio Spurs. He hit 11 of 19 from the field and had 5 points during a Suns 12–0 run in the fourth quarter. Kidd also had 5 assists and 10 rebounds. His preference is to hit the open man, but during this game his own shooting was hot. His offensive and defensive play gave the Suns the 94–81 victory.

Kidd continued to make a statement against his former team. On March 15, 1999, the Mavericks were once again his target. Kidd made several plays to help the Suns win. He caught a lob pass from Rex Chapman and put up a reverse dunk. He also hit a nineteen-foot jumper in the third quarter that sparked a 12–0 run by the Suns. Said Dallas guard Khalid Reeves of Kidd, "He really made things happen out there on the floor."[10] Kidd produced another triple double against the Mavs, with 20 points, 13 rebounds, 5 steals, 2 blocks, and 12 assists. The final score was 100–90, Suns.

Kidd was named NBA Player of the Week for the week ending March 15. The Suns won all four games for the week, as Kidd averaged 16 points, 10 assists, 6.5 rebounds, and 3 steals.

Kidd's passing ability caught the attention of not

Jason Kidd's wife, Joumana, encouraged her husband to improve his shooting percentage. She kept files that charted his progress in comparison to some of the league's top players, including Anfernee Hardaway and Gary Payton.

only fans but also advertisers. During the season, the Nike shoe company ran a series of commercials called the Fun Police. Jason Kidd, Damon Stoudamire, and Gary Payton were some of the guards featured as members of the Fun Police. In the commercials, the Fun Police would find players who did not pass the ball and try to convince them that passing is a fundamental part of the game.

Jason Kidd is a great competitor. His awareness of what is happening on the court allows him to find ways to get to the basket, either by putting up a shot or by passing the ball to a teammate so that someone else can make the shot.

Kidd exhibited his many talents when the Utah Jazz came to Phoenix to play the Suns on April 17, 1998. This game was very important to each team because the winner would have home-court advantage in the upcoming playoffs. The first quarter set the stage for the type of game it would be—a fast-paced, highly intense contest.

During the first half, the Suns were playing their fast-tempo brand of basketball. They were leading, 19–14, with nearly four minutes left in the first period. Kidd already had 3 assists. Rex Chapman, Kevin Johnson, and George McCloud were his targets. But the powerful duo of Jason Kidd and Antonio McDyess made several plays during the first half that displayed the quickness and control of the Suns. In one play, Kidd ran down the court and lobbed a perfectly positioned ball into the hands of McDyess. McDyess finished the play with a forceful slam dunk.

During the first half, the Suns were also able to capitalize on missed opportunities by the Jazz. With seconds left in the first quarter, point guard Howard Eisley of the Jazz dribbled down the lane and lost his footing and control of the ball. He recovered the ball and attempted an unbalanced lay-up. He missed the shot. The Jazz rebounded the ball twice at the hoop but failed to score. McCloud recovered the loose ball and flung the ball into Kidd's hands. Kidd raced downcourt and threw a no-look pass to McDyess. McDyess finished the play by flying over Karl Malone for a slam dunk. The crowd in the arena went wild, as the exciting first quarter came to an end. The Suns were up, 30–23, and Jason Kidd already had 7 assists.

As the second half began, the stage was set for Kidd to display his other skills. As one TNT commentator pointed out, "Not only does he push the ball up and has such tremendous court vision, but . . . he's so quick getting to the rim."[11]

The tempo at the beginning of the third quarter was slow, with technical fouls and missed passes.

FACT

Jason Kidd's favorite movie is *A Bronx Tale*. His favorite actor is Robert DeNiro, and his favorite actress is Julia Roberts.

Neither team made a statement, but this did not last long. With the Spurs up by four points, 58–54, Kidd was fouled. He made both foul shots. To top it off, he deflected the inbound pass. It was recovered by the Spurs for a split second but lost. Kidd recovered the loose ball and put in the lay-up for a total of 4 unanswered points within seconds.

At the end of the third quarter, the Suns led, 78–73. In the fourth quarter, both teams felt the urgency to win. Within seconds, Karl Malone made a two-point jumper. With 7:36 to go in the game, the Jazz led, 84–82. Kidd dished a kick pass to McCloud, who stylishly put in the three-pointer that electrified the crowd and tied the score at 88–88. The teams continued to trade shots. Karl Malone put in a turn-around jumper, and Kidd responded by putting in an off-balance alley-oop lay-up, to tie the score at 92–92.

Momentum swayed in favor of the Jazz when John Stockton covered Kevin Johnson and forced a turnover. The Jazz put in two baskets for a 96–92 lead. The Suns had possession of the ball and called a timeout to regroup. Kidd passed to McCloud, who put up a shot, but it did not fall. Kidd nabbed the rebound and hoisted a quick pass to Chapman, who put in a three-point jumper.

With 1:30 remaining, the Jazz led, 98–95; with 28

Jason Kidd's marketability has led to roles in many Nike commercials. One ad campaign featured Kidd and other guards such as Damon Stoudamire and Gary Payton as the Fun Police. They talked about the importance of passing.

seconds left, the score was 101–97, Jazz in front. The Suns went to Kidd for a quick lay-up. Karl Malone threw the inbound pass to Jeff Hornacek. The Suns tried to foul, but Utah was prepared for that strategy. Hornacek avoided the foul by running down the lane. Then he passed to John Stockton, who passed the ball to Bryon Russell. It took eight seconds, but the Suns finally fouled Bryon Russell. Russell went to the foul line and missed his first free throw. He regrouped and made the second free throw. The score was 102–99, Jazz. The Suns still had hope. Jason Kidd ran downcourt and delivered a pass to Cliff Robinson. But while driving to the basket, Robinson lost control. The Jazz recovered, and in the last three seconds they played keep-away, to win. The Jazz would have home-court advantage throughout the playoffs.

Jason Kidd continued to make things happen, however. In the last week of regular season, he was again named NBA Player of the Week—this time for the week ending April 19, 1998. He led the Suns to three of four wins, shot 49 percent, averaged 17.3 points, 11 assists, 8.3 rebounds, and 4 steals.

In the regular-season finale against the Houston Rockets, the Suns played like a playoff team. The win helped give the Suns home-court advantage for Games 1 and 2 in the first round of the playoffs; and if the series came down to the wire, Game 5 would be in Phoenix. The Suns were led by Jason Kidd and Cliff Robinson. Kidd played with intensity in the final game, and the Suns hoped that he would keep it up in the playoffs. Kidd's numbers for the game were 27 points, 4 steals, 8 rebounds, and 7 assists. The final score was 123–93, Suns. The Suns ended the regular season with a record of 56 wins and 26 losses—their first winning season since 1994–95; and the fourth-best finish in Suns history. In addition, they set a league record by holding opponents to 41.1 percent shooting.

Jason Kidd ended the regular season ranked number one in the NBA in triple doubles with 4, and second in assists with 9.1 per game. In addition, Kidd was the only Sun to appear and start in all 82 games during the season.

Chapter 7

Another Playoff Run

The Suns met the San Antonio Spurs in the first round of the playoffs. The Spurs knew that they had to contain Kidd. Coach Greg Popovich said, "Nobody is going to stop Jason. He's right in the top echelon of guards in this league."[1]

The first game was held on April 23, 1998. In the first quarter the Suns and the Spurs were answering each other with shots. Kidd helped the Suns break away by scoring 7 points in the second period, to give the Suns a 50–45 halftime lead. The 1996–1997 Rookie of the Year, Tim Duncan, made his playoff debut. The Suns were able to limit Duncan to 4 points in the first half. But he was able to adjust to the game, scoring the final 8 points for the Spurs in the third quarter. Despite Duncan's efforts, however, the Suns led, 75–67. Duncan relied on David Robinson to fake the Suns out so he could convert his shots. In the fourth quarter, he scored 6 points, to help the Spurs to an 84–83 lead. With less than two minutes left, Kidd had a steal and a lay-up, to bring the score to 96–92. He stole the ball again, which led to a foul on Kevin Johnson. Johnson could not find the basket and missed both free throws. With less than 30 seconds left, Duncan missed two free throws, and Johnson put in two foul shots, giving the Spurs a three-point lead. Avery Johnson of the Spurs made a free throw, and Duncan recovered the ball after Dennis Scott missed a three-pointer. Duncan hit two free throws, to give the Spurs the 102–96 victory.

In the first game of the playoffs, Kidd led both teams in assists with 11 and in steals with 6. He also posted 6 rebounds and put in 17 points. Kidd's reaction to the game: "Coming down the stretch, they made baskets when they had to, and we missed some that we normally make, so that's when the tide turned."[2] Said Kidd of his Rookie of the Year counterpart, "He [Duncan] made some tough shots and you have to give him credit. They called his number and he answered."[3] The Suns knew that they would have to come up with a different game plan to defend Duncan.

In the second game on April 25, 1998, the Suns put in their big men, George McCloud, Mark Bryant, and Antonio McDyess, to stop Tim Duncan and David Robinson. The Suns double-teamed, and sometimes triple-teamed, the duo. This defense held the duo to scoring zero points in the first quarter. With 10:27 left in the second quarter, Duncan scored. Sixty-eight seconds later, Robinson scored on a pair of free throws. The ability to stop Duncan and Robinson helped give the Suns a 51–47 halftime lead. Cliff Robinson opened the third quarter with a lay-up, and McCloud put up a three-pointer. Kidd made a catlike steal and two free throws to make the score 58–48 with 10:34 left. The Spurs battled back, coming within 7 points, but McDyess widened the lead by scoring 6 points in a row. At the end of three quarters, the Suns led, 83–71. The Spurs kept clawing at the lead. Duncan heightened the tension by putting in a six-footer. With 22 seconds remaining, the score was 103–101, Suns. The Suns put the brakes on the Spurs. Rex Chapman was fouled with 12 seconds remaining. He made one of two. Jared Jackson of the Spurs tried for a three-pointer to tie the score, but the shot did not fall. Mark Bryant iced the win by putting in 4 free throws. The final score

In his second season with Phoenix, Jason Kidd once again led the Suns to the playoffs. This time around, the Suns faced David Robinson, Tim Duncan, and the San Antonio Spurs.

was 108–101. Kidd finished with 12 points and once again led both teams in assists with 10 and in steals with 3. The series was tied at two.

Duncan and Robinson adjusted to the Suns' defense and combined for 13 points in the first quarter, giving the Spurs a 20–17 lead at the end of the quarter. The Spurs led by 7 points midway through the second quarter, but the Suns took it up several notches, pulling to a 44–44 tie at halftime. In the third quarter, the Spurs took the lead. They established a slow pace, which was the opposite of how the Suns wanted to play. With 8:38 left in the period, the Spurs led, 54–48. With 7:17 remaining, the Suns cut the lead to 56–52 with a thunderous dunk by McCloud. But the Spurs went on an 11–3 burst that gave them a 12-point lead going into the fourth quarter. They had limited the Suns to scoring just 15 points in the third. Jared Jackson made up for his missed three-pointer during Game 2. He shot six of eight from the field and was instrumental throughout the game. He hit a three-pointer with 3:38 left in the game. The Suns came within 10 points, but the final score was 100–88, Spurs. The Spurs led the series, 2 games to 1. Jason Kidd had 16 points, 12 rebounds, 6 assists, and 3 steals. If Kidd and the Suns had any hope of moving to round two, they had to regroup. Said Kidd of the loss,

FACT

Jason Kidd started collecting baseball cards when he was in elementary school. He and his friends tried to collect all of the players in the major leagues. Today his "collection" has grown to include a bat autographed by Ken Griffey, Jr.

They made their shots and we didn't. They got on us and we didn't respond in the third. That was the turning point. But Wednesday is a whole new day and a whole new game. We've been together long enough to pull together. This team has the confidence to do that when our backs are up against the wall. This series isn't over.[4]

Going into Game 4, the Suns were without two of their big men due to injuries—Danny Manning had a knee injury and Rex Chapman had a hamstring injury. The Suns' strategy was to double-team Duncan and Robinson. Coach Ainge thought that doing so would help shut down the Spurs. After all, that game plan worked in Game 2. Doing so, however, left Avery Johnson open and gave him the opportunity to make plays. Avery Johnson would spell the demise of the Suns. He was able to stop the run of the Suns. Johnson and the Spurs made their run in the third quarter.

Again in the third quarter, the Spurs were able to stop the Suns. Kevin Johnson put in two baskets, to bring the Suns within one point with 2:39 to play in the third quarter. However, Avery Johnson's lay-up sparked the Spurs to a 9–3 run. Said Kidd after the game, "It seemed like there was a lid on the basket at times tonight."[5] The Spurs were up, 62–55, going into the fourth quarter. They rallied for a 22–2 run

Despite his best efforts, Jason Kidd could not lead the Suns past the Spurs in the first round of the 1998 playoffs.

that crushed the hopes of the Suns. Avery Johnson finished the game with 30 points. Kidd called Johnson "the engine that runs that machine."[6] For his ability to shut down the Suns, Avery Johnson was named the NBA Most Valuable Player. The Suns had a shooting percentage of 36.8. For the third straight postseason, the Suns were unable to reach the second level. The mission for the Suns during the off-season was to find a way to elevate to the second round of the playoffs and beyond.

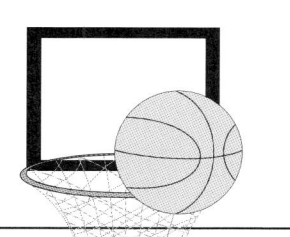

Chapter 8
The Kidd's Bright Future

On July 1, 1998, the National Basketball Association (NBA) announced a lockout, putting a halt to the 1998–1999 season. There was a collective lock on all the arenas around the league—a lock that prevented the players from entering any arena and from playing professional basketball.

Owners of NBA teams believed the players received more money than the owners. The owners wanted to restrict the amount of money the players made—leaving more profit for the owners. During the lockout, however, there would be no games played—no money made by or for anyone.

There had been two other lockouts in NBA history—one in 1995 and one in 1996. Neither lockout lasted longer than three months. But this lockout was destined to last longer. Negotiations took place between the owners and representative players. Several meetings occurred between July 1 and November 3, the scheduled season opener. But a decision was not reached.

Most players agreed that they wanted the lockout to be lifted so that they could play basketball. One of the players who wanted very much to be able to play was Jason Kidd. Considered the key player for the Suns, Kidd's sudden impact on the team had changed players and fans alike. Would Kidd and the Suns have the opportunity to showcase their talents and play in the upcoming season?

Jason Kidd kept in shape during the lockout. He spent time in the weight room and added muscle to his frame. Already considered one of the strongest point guards in the NBA, he wanted to ensure that he had advantages over smaller guards in half-court defenses.

Meanwhile, Jason Kidd and his wife, Joumana, celebrated the birth of their first child, Trey Jason (T.J.) Kidd, on October 12, 1998. The potential point guard weighed nine pounds, two ounces, and was twenty-two inches long. One positive element of the strike-shortened 1998 NBA season was that Kidd had the opportunity to spend more time with his family.

The Player's Association and the owners were not making any headway in negotiations. Things were looking so bad that NBA commissioner David Stern suggested that replacement players would be used for the 1999–2000 season if the conflict was not resolved soon.

On January 6, 1999, player representative Billy Hunter and Commissioner Stern held an all-night meeting in an attempt to get the players back on the court. They reached a compromise. After a short training camp, an abbreviated season would begin February 1, 1999.

The players were pleased with the agreement but worried about fan reaction. After all, the average player is a millionaire and the average owner is a billionaire, and the lockout and publicity surrounding it brought salaries to the public's attention.

Now it was time for mending any resentment that fans felt. Jason Kidd looked for reactions from the players. Said Kidd, "An apology is in order."[1] He hoped that fans would be understanding.

The Suns tried to lessen the distance between the team and its fans. They invited fans to attend a scrimmage game. Approximately six thousand fans showed up. They were given free popcorn, soft

FACT

Jason Kidd has a picture of a black panther tattooed on his chest. He chose a panther because it is sleek, fast, and very powerful—all qualities that Kidd wants to bring to his game.

drinks, T-shirts, and basketballs. As an added bonus, Cliff Robinson, Luc Longley, and Jason Kidd threw their sneakers into the crowd.

Once the lockout ended, the Suns were able to add to their lineup. They acquired center Luc Longley and Tom Gugliotta. Longley brought his passing skills and experience in winning championships with Michael Jordan and the Chicago Bulls; and Gugliotta brought good inside and outside shooting.

Gone from the club was Kevin Johnson. Johnson decided to retire after the 1997–1998 season. He passed the leadership role on the court and in the locker room to Jason Kidd.

After the first few games of the regular season, attendance at the America West Arena began to reach normal levels. As of February 19, 1999, the Suns' record was 5–3. The team tried to improve its record when it faced the Detroit Pistons. It was a face-off between the former corookies of the year.

The Pistons started playing a defensive game in the opening seconds. The Suns could not find a rhythm and demonstrated sloppy play. No matter what they tried, the ball had a hard time finding the basket. Alvin Gentry, coach of the Pistons, had a game plan that was working. He wanted to contain Kidd in the first half, and that is exactly what the

After a lockout cancelled the first three months of the 1998–99 NBA season, Jason Kidd sympathized with the fans. He said, "An apology is in order."

Pistons did. However, in their rush to contain Kidd, the Pistons fouled him several times. Most of the points in the first quarter for the Suns came from Jason Kidd's taking aim from the foul line. At the end of the first quarter, the score was 27–15, Pistons. This was the lowest scoring quarter of the abbreviated season for the Suns.

In the second quarter the Suns found their rhythm. The team came on with a run that was highlighted by a three-point play from George McCloud. In the last four minutes of the quarter, the Suns went on a 22–6 run. The end of this quarter was highlighted by an incredible play by Jason Kidd. On a fast break, Kidd streamed down the lane, put up a touch pass, and scored, tying the game at 46 at the half.

As the third quarter progressed, Jason Kidd put a shutter-step lay-up to the glass, to give the Suns a 62–58 lead. He also put up a three-pointer from the perimeter. He was wide open because the defense thought the outside shot was his weakness. This is one area in which Kidd had improved during the off-season.

Detroit wanted to snap a five-game losing streak. As the fourth quarter was winding down, Detroit's defense took control. The Suns could not get their running game back on track. The Pistons showed patience in playing their type of ball. The final score was 101–93, Pistons.

One element that Coach Ainge noticed that needed work was the Suns' ability to maintain their intensity into the third quarter. The downward trend began in the second quarter and continued. Ainge did not attribute the problem to the lockout or to the lack of training-camp time. He just reminded the team that it was embarrassing to have the lead in a game and then lose it. He hoped that the embarrassment factor would motivate the players.

In the first month of the abbreviated fifty-game season, Jason Kidd had already posted his fourth triple double in a 94–96 win over the Vancouver Grizzlies on February 25, 1999, by logging 14 points, 16 assists, and 12 rebounds. Kidd was ranked first in the league for triple doubles. The Suns had won all games in which Kidd posted a triple double. He also ranked first in assists per game with 11.8, and had a season high of 18 assists against the Golden State Warriors on February 25, 1999.

This momentum carried Jason Kidd into finishing with the season of his career. In fifty games, he averaged 16.9 points, 10.8 assists, 6.8 rebounds, and 2.28 steals. With these numbers, Kidd surpassed his averages in scoring, assists, and rebounds in a season. The last player to accomplish

Since being traded to the Suns, Jason Kidd has had plenty of reasons to smile.

this was Kidd's idol, Magic Johnson, during the 1990–91 season. This stellar season performance was a true testament to Kidd's being selected as a member of the 2000 Olympic team for the United States.

Michael Jordan announced his retirement from basketball after the lockout was settled. Although many players and fans believe Jordan will always be the ambassador for basketball, many wondered who would be the one to bring the fans back and keep the excitement level high. Jason Kidd is considered a superstar on the verge of greatness. The feats he has accomplished while beginning his fifth season in the league are a good indication of what he can and will do. Kidd still remembers the summer of 1996, when Michael Jordan took the time to speak with him about handling fame and the pressures that go with playing basketball, and answered the questions that Kidd had. Their conversation lasted forty-five minutes, and Kidd absorbed all of Jordan's advice.

Jason Kidd is a true impact player. His presence elevates his team to another level. His aggressive style of play, fearlessness on the drive, and the pressure he puts on the other team have led the Suns to make defense a fundamental part of their game.

One way that players become superstars is by finding ways to win, and that is always on Kidd's mind at game time. "My job is to win ballgames, help the team win."[2]

Coach Ainge knows Jason Kidd has superstar potential. He said of Kidd, "If he ever completely fulfills his leadership capabilities and develops a better shot, he can be a superstar."[3] The conditions are perfect for Jason Kidd to lead the Suns into the new millennium.

Chapter Notes

Chapter 1. Giving 100 Percent

1. "Kidd Unstoppable as Suns Roll Past Rockets," *The Sporting News* Online, April 25, 1999, <http://tsn.sportingnews.com/nba/scoreboard/19990425/recap/156029.html> (June 8, 1999).

2. Jason Kidd's Official Web site, June 8, 1999, <http://www.jasonkidd.net/player/latest.html> (June 10, 1999).

Chapter 2. Evolution of a Point Guard

1. Phil Taylor, "NCAA Preview: One Day With Jason," *Sports Illustrated* electronic library March 21, 1994, <http://elibrary.com/education> (January 19, 1999).

2. Ibid.

3. Jeramie McKeep, "Just Kiddin'," *Fastbreak Magazine* Online, ©1997 NBA Properties, <http://www.nba.com/suns/00382578.html> (February 17, 1999).

4. Phil Taylor, "Inside High School Basketball: Jason Kidd," *Sports Illustrated*, February 18, 1991, p. 54.

5. Ibid.

6. Phil Taylor, "NCAA Preview: One Day With Jason," *Sports Illustrated* electronic library, March 21, 1994, <http://elibrary.com/education> (January 19, 1999).

7. Jeramie McKeep, "Just Kiddin'," *Fastbreak Magazine* Online, ©1997 NBA Properties, <http://www.nba.com/suns/00382578.html> (February 17, 1999).

8. Ibid.

9. Jim Thomas, "California Golden Bears Cal Quickly Discovered This Kidd's a Keeper," *St. Louis Post-Dispatch*, March 25, 1993, p. 5C.

10. Ibid.

Chapter 3. College Hoops

1. Ron Bergman, "Kidd Steals the Show in Cal Debut," *San Jose Mercury News*, December 2, 1992, p. 5D.

2. John Biever, "The NCAA," *Sports Illustrated*, March 29, 1993, p. 16.

3. John Akers, "Sweet 16 Sour for Cal, Stanford; Bears Are Left in Tears," *San Jose Mercury News*, March 26, 1993, p. 1G.

4. "College Basketball Kidd Stars as Cal Stuns No. 1 UCLA," *Newsday*, January 31, 1994, p. 90.

5. Greg Logan, "NCAA Tournament/West Regional Style Points Don't Count, Cal," *Newsday*, March 18, 1994, p. 210.

6. John Akers, "NBA Gains a Pair of Showstoppers; Kidd Leaves: I Felt My Job Here at Cal Was About Finished," *San Jose Mercury News*, March 24, 1994, p. 1G.

7. Ibid.

8. Ibid.

9. Michael J. Goodman, "Getting the Point: Dallas Mavericks New Point Guard Jason Kidd" *The Sporting News*, October 3, 1994, p. 47.

10. Ibid.

Chapter 4. Drafted by the Mavericks

1. Michael J. Goodman, "Getting the Point: Dallas Mavericks New Point Guard Jason Kidd," *The Sporting News*, October 3, 1994, p. 47.

2. Richard O'Brien and Franz Lidz, "Scorecard: The Dallas Mavericks Made Point Guard Jason Kidd the Second Pick," *Sports Illustrated*, August 1, 1994, p. 9.

3. "Still Mavericks (Dallas Mavericks 1994 draft)," *The Sporting News* electronic library, © 1994, <http://www.elibrary.com/education> (January 25, 1999).

4. The News and Observer Publishing Co. and the Associated Press (Dallas), electronic library, November 5, 1994, <http://work.nando.net/newsroom/basketball/1994/nba/archive/game/110594.html> (January 25, 1999).

5. Ibid.

6. Ibid.

7. Steve Aschburner, "Kidd's Stuff Makes Wolves Losers," *Minneapolis Star Tribune*, April 8, 1995, p. 1C.

8. *Associated Press*, "NBA Kidd's Big Game Lifts Mavs; Spurs' Win Streak Broken," *San Francisco Chronicle*, April 12, 1995, sports, p. 1D.

9. Steve Aschburner, "Rookie Race a Dogfight/Robinson, Kidd, Hill Stake Claims," *Minneapolis Star Tribune*, April 14, 1995, p. 1C.

10. *Associated Press*, "Mavericks' Kidd, Pistons' Hill Share NBA Rookie-of-Year Award," *The Los Angeles Times*, May 18, 1995, sports, p. 4.

11. "Jason's Lyric (Dallas Mavericks' Jason Kidd)" *The Sporting News*, electronic library, © 1995, <http://www.elibrary.com/education> (January 19, 1999).

12. Phil Taylor, "Pro Basketball: Agony of Defeat Dissension and Drink Have Threatened to Turn Dallas' Season Into a Debacle," *Sports Illustrated*, December 18, 1995, p. 34.

13. Ibid.

14. Chris Baker, "Kidd Shows Clippers Some of His Magic," *The Los Angeles Times,* January 31, 1996, p. 3.

15. Associated Press electronic library, "Dallas, Kidd Shows Stockton-Like Traits," April 7, 1997, <http://www.nando.net> (November 4, 1998).

16. Associated Press electronic library, "Kidd Proves He Belongs in All-Star Game," February 9, 1996, <http://www.nando.net> (November 4, 1998).

17. Ibid.

18. Ibid.

19. Ibid.

20. Scott Howard-Cooper, "Magic Gets His Hooks in Dallas," *The Los Angeles Times,* February 17, 1996, p. 1.

21. Johnette Howard, "The Ball's in His Hands," *Sports Illustrated,* January 11, 1996, p. 95.

22. Jorge L. Oritz, "Trade Creates a Beautiful Sun-rise for Kidd's Career," *San Francisco Chronicle,* December 29, 1996, p. D3.

Chapter 5. The Impact Player

1. Jackie MacMullan, "Hail and Good Riddance," *Sports Illustrated,* January 13, 1997, p. 87.

2. Associated Press and Dallas Morning News, "Kidd: A Ray of Sun Shine?" *The Seattle Times Online,* December 27, 1996, <http://libraries.wnec.edu/libraries/U.S.-newspaper.html> (April 23, 1998).

3. Bob Young, "New Bride Is Kidd's Highlight of the Day," *The Arizona Republic* Online, February 22, 1997, <http://www.azcentral.com/> (June 19, 1999).

4. *Mercury News Wire Services,* "Down 27 in Dallas, Kidd, Suns Win: Sonics, Payton, Top Magic," *San Jose Mercury News,* March 3, 1997, p. 8D.

5. Ibid.

6. Bob Young, "Kidd Excited Over Prospect of First Playoffs: Rocket Will Try to Slow Suns Run," *The Arizona Republic* Online, April 12, 1997, <http://www.azcentral.com/> (May 5, 1998).

7. Greg Boeck, "KJ and the Suns Shine," *USA Today*, April 22, 1997, p. 1C.

8. Ibid.

9. Bob Young, "Supersonics Get Mad, Then Get Even in Series," *The Arizona Republic* Online, April 28, 1997, <http://www.azcentral.com/> (May 6, 1998).

10. Bob Young, "See You Back in Seattle Dispute Heroics by Chapman, Suns Fall in OT," *The Arizona Republic* Online, May 2, 1997, <http://www.azcentral.com/> (May 7, 1998).

11. Bob Young, "Kidd Keeps Teenage Promise," *The Arizona Republic* Online, May 25, 1997, <http://www.azcentral.com/> (May 25, 1998).

Chapter 6. A Classic Point Guard

1. Jackie MacMullan, "In the Air With Jason Kidd," *Sports Illustrated*, January 1998, p. 54.

2. "Mrs. Assistant Coach," *Minneapolis Star Tribune*, November 30, 1997, p. 15C.

3. Ibid.

4. "Sunday Special: Inside NBA: NBA Western Conference: Midwest," *The Atlanta Journal and Constitution* electronic library, © 1997, <http://www.elibrary.com/education> (January 19, 1999).

5. Jim Gray, *NBC Sports Commentary, Half-Time Report*, interview with Jason Kidd during 1998 playoffs, April 1998.

6. Greg Boeck, "Suns Find This Kidd Something Special," *USA Today*, January 9, 1998, p. 11C.

7. Ibid.

8. Bob Young, "Mind Games," *The Sporting News* electronic library, © 1998, <http://www.elibrary.com/education> (January 19, 1999).

9. Norm Frauenheim, "Kidd's All-Star Spot Reflects Maturation," *The Arizona Republic* Online, January 29, 1998, <http://www.azcentral.com/> (May 3, 1998).

10. Bob Young, "Kidd Sends Mavericks A Message Delivers Triple Double," *The Arizona Republic Online*, March 16, 1998, <http://www.azcentral.com/> (May 6, 1998).

11. Cheryl Miller, *The NBA on TNT*, Utah Jazz versus Phoenix Suns, April 17, 1998.

Chapter 7. Another Playoff Run

1. Mel Reisner, "Kidd Holds Key to Sun's Advancing," *Associated Press* electronic library, April 1998, <http://www.elibrary.com/education> (January 19, 1999).

2. *ESPN Sports Zone*, "NBA Playoffs, San Antonio 102, Phoenix 96", April 23, 1998, <http://espn.go.com/nba/playoffs/quarterfinals/index.html> (February 10, 1999).

3. Ibid.

4. *ESPN Sports Zone*, "NBA Playoffs, Spurs Show They Can Play Small Ball, Beat Suns," April 27, 1998, <http://espn.go.com/nba/playoffs/quarterfinals/index.html> (February 10, 1999).

5. *ESPN Sports Zone*, "Avery Plays a Very Big Role in Series Win," April 27, 1998, <http://espn.go.com/nba/playoffs/quarterfinals/index.htm> (February 10, 1999).

6. Ibid.

Chapter 8. The Kidd's Bright Future

1. Norm Frauenheim and Bob Young, "Players Prepared to See Resentment From Fans, Rookies Relieved Careers Finally Will Get Started," *Arizona Republic Online*, May 6, 1998, <http://www.azcentral.com/> (January 7, 1999).

2. Dan Bickley, "Kidd's Time to Shine Like Mike Arrives," *Arizona Republic Online*, May 23, 1998, <http://www.azcentral.com/> (February 20, 1999).

3. Norm Frauenheim, "Kidd's All-Star Shot Reflects Maturation," *Arizona Republic* Online, January 28, 1998, <http://www.azcentral.com/> (May 5, 1998).

Career Statistics

Year	Team	G	FG%	REB	AST	STL	BLK	PTS
1994–95	Mavericks	79	.385	430	607	151	24	922
1995–96	Mavericks	81	.381	553	783	175	26	1,348
1996–97	Mavericks/Suns	55	.403	249	496	124	20	599
1997–98	Suns	82	.416	510	745	162	26	954
1998–99	Suns	50	.444	339	539	114	19	846
Totals		347	.397	2,081	3,170	726	115	4,669

G—Games **FG%**—Field Goal Percentage **REB**—Rebounds
AST—Assists **STL**—Steals **BLK**—Blocks **PTS**—Points

Where to Write Jason Kidd

Mr. Jason Kidd
c/o Phoenix Suns
American West Arena
201 E. Jefferson St.
Phoenix, AZ 85004

On the Internet at:

Jason Kidd's Official Web Site
<http://www.jasonkidd.net/>

Phoenix Suns' Official Web Site
<http://www.nba.com/suns/index.html>

Index

A
Aikman, Troy, 33
Ainge, Danny, 51–52, 55, 58, 65, 80, 91

B
Baker, Vin, 9
Barkley, Charles, 8, 44–45
Beard, Butch, 36
Bird, Larry, 40, 65–66
Bozeman, Todd, 26, 30
Bryant, Mark, 77

C
Campanelli, Lou, 20, 22, 25–26
Carter, Donald, 33, 34
Cassell, Sam, 49
Chapman, Rex, 9, 55–56, 58, 67, 69, 77, 80
Cleamons, Jim, 48
Cornwell, Andre, 20
Cow Palace, 23, 25

D
Drexler, Clyde, 44–45
Dumas, Tony, 49
Duncan, Tim, 9, 75–76

E
Eisley, Howard, 70

F
Finley, Michael, 49
Fun Police, The, 69

G
Garnett, Kevin, 9
Gentry, Alvin, 89
Green, A.C., 49
Gugliotta, Tom, 9, 86

H
Haase, Jerod, 23
Hardaway, Penny, 62
Hardaway, Tim, 9
Hendrick, Brian, 22
Hill, Grant, 35, 39, 40, 62
Hornacek, Jeff, 73
Houston, Allan, 9
Hunter, Billy, 85
Hurley, Billy, 26

J
Jackson, Jared, 77, 79
Jackson, Jim, 35–36, 40
Johnson, Avery, 76, 80, 82
Johnson, Earvin "Magic," 16, 25, 40, 43, 46, 89
Johnson, Frank, 62–63
Johnson, Kevin, 52, 56, 62, 69, 71, 76, 80, 86
Jones, Eddie, 66
Jordan, Michael, 45, 59, 66, 90

K
Karl, George, 56
Kemp, Shawn, 44, 55
Kidd, Anne, 13
Kidd, Steve, 13, 31, 48
Kidd, Trey Jason, 84

L
LaPorte, Frank, 16-17
Leventhal, Don, 34
lockout, 83–84
Longley, Luc, 86

M
Malone, Karl, 59, 71
Manning, Danny, 8
Martin, Darrick, 62

Mashburn, Jamal, 35, 39–40
McCloud, George, 59, 69–71, 77, 88
McDyess, Antonio, 59, 69–70
Meyer, Loren, 49
Mobley, Cuttino, 8
Motta, Dick, 34, 35, 40
Murray, Lamond, 23, 26

N
National Basketball Association (NBA)
  NBA All-Star Game, 44–45, 66
  NBA Commissioner, 85
  NBA Player of the Month, 38
  NBA Player of the Week, 67, 73
National Collegiate Athletic Association (NCAA), 26–28
Nash, Steve, 62–63

O
Oakland Coliseum Arena, 17, 23, 36
Olajuwon, Hakeem, 44

P
Payton, Gary, 9, 45, 55, 62, 69
Person, Wesley, 56
Pippen, Scottie, 7–8
Popovich, Greg, 75

R
Reeves, Khalid, 67
Robinson, Cliff, 77, 86
Robinson, David, 76–77
Robinson, Glenn, 35, 39
Russell, Bryon, 73

S
Samaha, Joumana, 53, 62, 84
Scott, Dennis, 76
Schremp, Detlef, 55
Schuler, Mike, 38
Silas, Paul, 53
Smith, Emmitt, 33
Smith, Steve, 9
Sonju, Norm, 35
Stern, David, 85
Stockton, John, 45, 59, 66, 71, 73
Stone, Kim, 17
Stoudamire, Damon, 69

T
Tisdale, Wayman, 53

U
USA Basketball Men's Senior National Team, 9

W
Walker, Herschel, 33
Walters, Rex 27